C000046216

This coloring book belongs to:

_____

Coloring life
All rights reserved

Let's start

coloring

END

Thank you ♥

Don't forget to visit
our store **"Coloring life"**
in Amazon

6 in x 9 in coloring books:
www.coloringlife50.wordpress.com
8.5 in x 11 in coloring books:
www.coloringlife50.wordpress.com/top

Coloring life
All rights reserved

Printed in Great Britain
by Amazon

19999307R00061